Dear Par...

Congratulation...
the first steps on an exc...
The destination? Independent read...

STEP INTO READING® will help your child get there. The program offers five steps to reading success. Each step includes fun stories and colorful art or photographs. In addition to original fiction and books with favorite characters, there are Step into Reading Non-Fiction Readers, Phonics Readers and Boxed Sets, Sticker Readers, and Comic Readers—a complete literacy program with something to interest every child.

Learning to Read, Step by Step!

Ready to Read   Preschool–Kindergarten
• big type and easy words • rhyme and rhythm • picture clues
For children who know the alphabet and are eager to begin reading.

Reading with Help   Preschool–Grade 1
• basic vocabulary • short sentences • simple stories
For children who recognize familiar words and sound out new words with help.

Reading on Your Own   Grades 1–3
• engaging characters • easy-to-follow plots • popular topics
For children who are ready to read on their own.

Reading Paragraphs   Grades 2–3
• challenging vocabulary • short paragraphs • exciting stories
For newly independent readers who read simple sentences with confidence.

Ready for Chapters   Grades 2–4
• chapters • longer paragraphs • full-color art
For children who want to take the plunge into chapter books but still like colorful pictures.

STEP INTO READING® is designed to give every child a successful reading experience. The grade levels are only guides; children will progress through the steps at their own speed, developing confidence in their reading. The F&P Text Level on the back cover serves as another tool to help you choose the right book for your child.

Remember, a lifetime love of reading starts with a single step!

Copyright © 2021 by Tad Hills
Text by Elle Stephens
Art by Grace Mills

All rights reserved. Published in the United States by Random House Children's Books, a division
of Penguin Random House LLC, New York.

Step into Reading, Random House, and the Random House colophon are registered trademarks of
Penguin Random House LLC.

Visit us on the Web!
StepIntoReading.com
rhcbooks.com

Educators and librarians, for a variety of teaching tools, visit us at RHTeachersLibrarians.com

Library of Congress Cataloging-in-Publication Data is available upon request.
ISBN 978-0-593-18122-5 (trade pbk.) — ISBN 978-0-593-18123-2 (lib. bdg.) —
ISBN 978-0-593-18125-6 (hardcover) — ISBN 978-0-593-18124-9 (ebook)

Printed in the United States of America
10 9 8 7 6 5 4 3 2 1

This book has been officially leveled by using the F&P Text Level Gradient™ Leveling System.

STEP INTO READING®

STEP 1 READY TO READ

Rocket Has a Sleepover

Pictures based on the art by Tad Hills

Random House 🏠 New York

Rocket is happy!

He is having a sleepover
with his friends.

The friends play
hide-and-seek.

They eat snacks.

Later,
they say
good night.

But Rocket
is not tired.
He can not sleep.

"I will tell you a story,"
says Fred.

"There once was a puppy
who loved to swim."

"One day,

he met a frog."

"Then what?"
asks Rocket.

Fred falls asleep!

Rocket is not tired.
"I will finish the story,"
says Owl.

"The puppy and the frog had a race."

"Who won?" asks Rocket.

Zzzzz . . .

Now Owl is
asleep!

Rocket is not tired.

"I will finish
the story,"
says Bella.

"The frog got tired
and needed to rest!"
says Bella.

"The frog called
for help."

"The puppy was about to win the race."

"Then what?"

asks Rocket.

Now Bella
is asleep!

"Oh no," says Rocket.
All his friends
are asleep.

"I will finish
the story,"
he says.

"The puppy
went back."

"He helped the frog."

"They finished
the race together,"
says Rocket.

"The frog and the puppy
were tired."

Rocket yawns.

"They found a blanket
and fell fast asleep.
The end."

Rocket is tired.

He falls fast asleep.

The end.